American edition published in 2000 by Carolrhoda Books, Inc., by arrangement
with Transworld Publishers Ltd., London, England.

Carolrhoda Books, Inc., a Division of Lerner Publishing Group
241 First Avenue North, Minneapolis, MN 55401 U.S.A.

Website address: www.lernerbooks.com

Library of Congress Cataloging-in-Publication Data

Haughton, Emma.
Rainy day / by Emma Haughton ; illustrated by Angelo Rinaldi.
p.   cm.
Summary: Shortly after his parents have separated, Nick visits his father
on a gray, rainy day and they take a long walk in the storm.
ISBN 1-57505-452-3 (alk. paper)
[1. Fathers and sons—Fiction. 2. Storms—Fiction. 3. Walking—Fiction]
I. Rinaldi, Angelo, ill. II. Title.
PZ7.H28675Rai   2000
[E]—dc21   99-38028

Printed in Singapore
1 2 3 4 5 6 05 04 03 02 01 00

Rainy Day

Emma Haughton *Illustrated by* Angelo Rinaldi

CAROLRHODA BOOKS, INC.
MINNEAPOLIS

The morning of the visit it began to rain. Nick sat in his dad's new apartment, watching the first splash of drops on the window. One by one they fell, fatter and faster, until he could hardly see through to the buildings across the street.

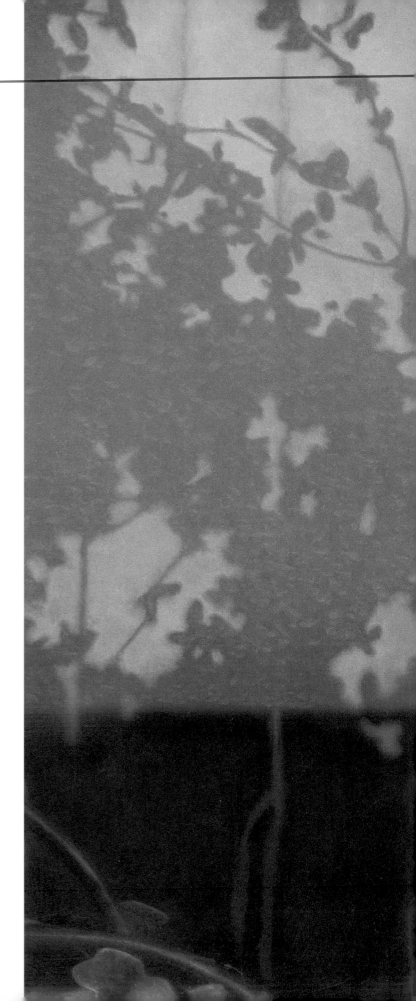

"Looks like the fair will have to wait until next week," said Dad.

"But you promised," said Nick.

"I'm sorry," said Dad. He put a hand on Nick's shoulder. "I was looking forward to it too, you know."

Nick shrugged and said nothing. He leaned his head against the window. It felt cold and hard. Raindrops trickled down the glass.

Dad grabbed Nick's coat and dropped it in his lap.

"Come on," he said. "We're off."

"Where?" asked Nick, not moving.

"I don't know," said Dad. "We'll see."

Down on the street, cars hissed past, water spraying up from their wheels. An old man struggled with an umbrella in the wind. A baby peered at Nick through the plastic bubble over its stroller.

N ick walked slowly, trying to keep his feet dry. Dad stopped and waited.

"Hang on," he said, and he dived into a store. He came out with a pair of rubber boots. "Try these." He pulled off Nick's shoes.

Nick scowled. "Too big."

Dad pressed the toes. "They'll do."

Nick stomped in every puddle, splashing dirty water everywhere. His jeans clung to his legs, cold and clammy. Suddenly the rain got heavier, hurtling out of the sky and stinging Nick's cheeks. His hair began to drip into his eyes.

Everywhere people rushed for cover, but Dad strode on.

When Nick got to the park, Dad was waiting.

"Look." Dad pointed to a trickle of rainwater running down through the trees. "A stream."

He picked up a stick and started to clear the leaves from its path. The water rushed and danced ahead. Nick ran to keep up.

"Here!" shouted Nick.

Near the drain was a large tangle of twigs and leaves. With a quick flick of his stick, Dad broke through the dam. The water surged forward and gurgled into the black, echoey depths below.

They followed the path through the trees as it curved toward the sea. A dog bounded out of nowhere and jumped up to lick Nick's face. Its damp fur smelled of old carpets.

"Jessie!" its owner yelled and tugged it away, but the dog broke free and skidded off into the downpour.

"You okay?" asked Dad, brushing the mud from Nick's coat.

Nick nodded. "Can we go and look at the sea?"

"Sure," said Dad. "Let's go."

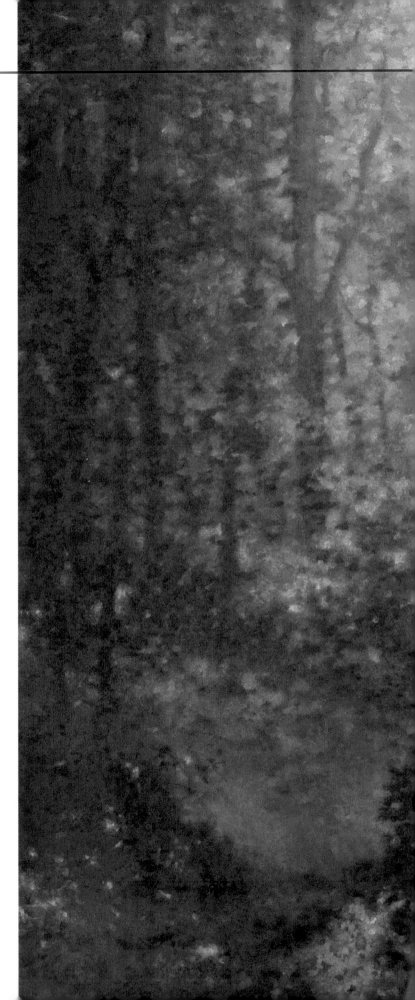

The seafront was empty. Clouds raced across the bay. The air smelled salty fresh. Waves swelled and heaved and crashed against the seawall, sending plumes of spray onto the stone walkway. They stood by the edge, dodging the water as it flew up around them. Nick laughed when Dad didn't get away in time.

Tired and soaked, they sat on a bench and watched the puddles of rain and spray flow back into the sea.

"Hungry?" asked Dad.

"Starving," said Nick.

Dad reached in his pocket and pulled out a small package of cookies. Most were broken, but they still tasted good.

Dad looked at Nick's wet clothes and muddy coat.

"Look at you," he said. "Your mom will kill me."

"She won't mind," said Nick, trying not to shiver, "as long as I'm all right."

"And are you?" asked Dad.

Suddenly the sun broke through the cover of gray.
The seagulls began to scream and swoop.
The tips of the waves sparkled in the bright light.

Nick blinked. "I miss you," he said.

"Me too," said Dad. "All the time."

He turned and gave Nick a long, hard squeeze.

"Things will get better," said Dad, "I promise."
Nick smiled. "I know," he said. "Rainy days aren't
so bad. And they don't last forever."